Mrs. Huggins and Her Hen Hannah

LYDIA DABCOVICH

E. P. DUTTON   NEW YORK

in memory of Norma Farber,
who gave Mrs. Huggins her name

Unicorn is a registered trademark of E. P. Dutton
Library of Congress number 85-4406
ISBN 0-525-44368-1
Published in the United States by E. P. Dutton,
2 Park Avenue, New York, N.Y. 10016,
a division of NAL Penguin Inc.
Published simultaneously in Canada by
Fitzhenry and Whiteside Limited, Toronto
Editor: Ann Durell   Designer: Edith T. Weinberg
Printed in Hong Kong by South China Printing Co.
First Unicorn Edition 1988   W
10 9 8 7 6 5 4 3 2 1

Mrs. Huggins lived with her hen Hannah.
Together they did everything.

They cooked and baked

and cleaned and scrubbed.

They did the wash

and hung it up to dry.

Together they planted,
raked and watered their garden,

and picked ripe apples and red tomatoes
for tasty pies and juicy stews.

Together they sheared the sheep

and milked the cow.

Every evening, by their warm fire,
they stitched and darned.

Then they yawned and stretched,
wound the clock, said good-night
and went to bed.

One day, Hannah got sick.

Mrs. Huggins nursed her day and night.

But very soon, Hannah died.
Mrs. Huggins was very sad.
She buried Hannah in a green meadow.

The cottage seemed very empty without
Hannah. Mrs. Huggins sat and cried.

Suddenly she heard a sound
from Hannah's nest.

And there was a fuzzy little chick.

Now Mrs. Huggins lives with
Hannah's daughter.

Together they do everything.